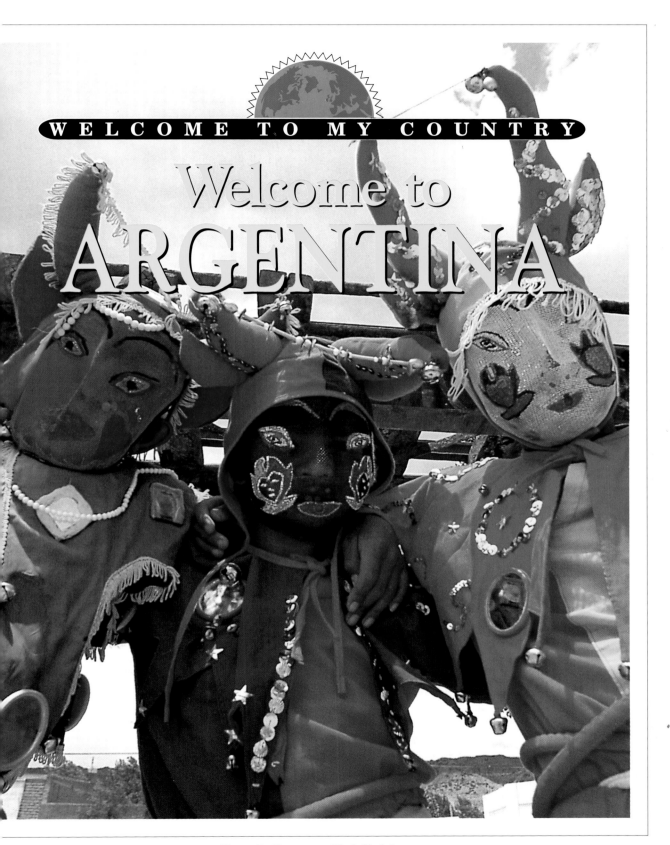

Welcome to
ARGENTINA

Gareth Stevens Publishing
A WORLD ALMANAC EDUCATION GROUP COMPANY

Written by
GERALDINE MESENAS/NICOLE FRANK

Designed by
LYNN CHIN

Picture research by
SUSAN JANE MANUEL

First published in North America in 2001 by
Gareth Stevens Publishing
A World Almanac Education Group Company
330 West Olive Street, Suite 100
Milwaukee, Wisconsin 53212 USA

For a free color catalog describing
Gareth Stevens' list of high-quality books
and multimedia programs, call
1-800-542-2595 (USA) or
1-800-461-9120 (CANADA).
Gareth Stevens Publishing's
Fax: (414) 332-3567.

© **TIMES EDITIONS PTE LTD 2001**
Originated and designed by
Times Editions
An imprint of Times Media Private Limited
A member of the Times Publishing Group
Times Centre, 1 New Industrial Road
Singapore 536196
http://www.timesone.com.sg/te

Library of Congress Cataloging-in-Publication Data
Mesenas, Geraldine.
Welcome to Argentina / Geraldine Mesenas and Nicole Frank.
p. cm.-- (Welcome to my country)
Includes bibliographical references and index.
ISBN 0-8368-2515-2 (lib. bdg.)
1. Argentina--Juvenile literature. [1. Argentina.]
I. Frank, Nicole. II. Title. III. Series.
F2808.2 .M47   2001
982--dc21   00-058326

Printed in Malaysia

1 2 3 4 5 6 7 8 9 05 04 03 02 01

PICTURE CREDITS
A.N.A. Press Agency: 14, 33 (top)
Giulio Andreini: 33 (bottom)
Archive Photos: 10, 13, 15 (both), 29,
    36 (top), 43
Sylvia Cordaiy Photo Library: 7
DDB Stock Photo: 39
Focus Team: 1, 2, 3 (center), 9 (bottom), 16, 18,
    28, 38 (both)
Eduardo Gil: 5, 22
HBL Network Photo Agency: 3 (bottom), 4, 19,
    36 (bottom), 37
Dave G. Houser Stock Photography: 17, 23, 31
The Hutchison Library: 6 (bottom), 21, 26, 32
Ira Rubin: 6 (top), 9 (top), 35 (bottom)
David Simson: 3 (top), 11, 20, 24, 25, 30, 40,
    41 (bottom), 45
South American Pictures: 34, 35 (top), 41 (top)
Tony Stone Images/Vision Photo Agency: cover
Trip Photographic Library: 8, 12, 27

Digital Scanning by Superskill Graphics Pte Ltd

Contents

Words that appear in the glossary are printed in **boldface** type the first time they occur in the text.

Welcome to Argentina!

Argentina is the eighth largest country in the world. Its length is 2,300 miles (3,701 kilometers), so it has many landscapes and climates. Let's explore this large country and learn about the Argentines and their **vibrant** culture!

Opposite: Mount Fitzroy in Santa Cruz province is a favorite with mountain climbers.

Below: Buenos Aires, the capital of Argentina, is the economic center of the country.

The Flag of Argentina

The national flag of Argentina has two blue bands and one white band. Blue represents the sky at midday in May, the month of Argentina's 1810 revolution. White stands for purity. The emblem is called the "Sun of May."

The Land

The land area of Argentina is large. It covers almost 1.1 million square miles (2.8 million square km). Bolivia and Paraguay are north of Argentina. Brazil and Uruguay lie to the northeast. Chile and the Andes Mountains are to the west, and the Atlantic Ocean is to the east. At 22,834 feet (6,960 meters), Argentina's Mount Aconcagua is the Western Hemisphere's highest peak.

Above: Iguazú Falls, situated along the Iguazú River, was made a World Heritage National Monument in 1984.

Left: The Andes Mountains form a natural border between Argentina and Chile.

Argentina has four land zones — the **pampas**, the northeastern plains, Patagonia, and the Andes Mountains. The grassy pampas are home to over half of Argentina's people. The hot, thorny Gran Chaco region is one part of the northeastern plains. The other part is Mesopotamia, located between the Paraná and Uruguay Rivers. The southern quarter of Argentina is Patagonia. Few people live there.

Above: Located in central Argentina, the pampas are covered with grasslands. Buenos Aires and other large cities are located in the pampas region.

Climate

Argentina and North America have seasons at opposite times. June to September is winter in Argentina, and December to March is summer. The climate of Argentina changes along its length. The northeastern regions have dry winters and humid, hot summers with heavy rains and temperatures as high as 120° Fahrenheit (49° Celsius). Southern Patagonia and the high Andes have very cold, windy winters. Eastern Patagonia is rocky desert.

Plants and Animals

Argentina's different landscapes allow many species of plants and animals to grow well. National parks also provide a **haven** for plants and animals.

Above: The rhea can grow to a height of 4 feet (1.2 m).

Unique plant and animal species include the *quebracho* (kay-BRA-cho) tree, which grows in the Chaco region; the rhea, which resembles an ostrich and lives in the pampas; and the capybara, the world's largest rodent.

History

Ancient peoples from Asia began to live in Argentina about 10,000 B.C.

In the sixteenth century, many European explorers arrived in Argentina. The first European to discover the area was the Spanish explorer Juan Díaz de Solís, who arrived in 1516. In 1536, explorer Pedro de Mendoza founded the city of Buenos Aires.

Left: Sebastian Cabot arrived in Argentina in 1526. He established the first Spanish settlement in the Río de la Plata region.

Native Indians attacked early European settlers. However, by the late 1700s, Buenos Aires was the capital of a large Spanish colony that sent trading ships to Europe. In the 1800s, British attacks on Buenos Aires were defeated. In Europe, Napoleon of France had removed Spain's king.

In Buenos Aires on May 25, 1810, the May Revolution created a new government in Argentina. It was less loyal to the powerless Spanish king. By July 1816, Argentina had declared its independence from Spain.

Prosperity and Depression

From 1880 to 1928, Argentina enjoyed a time of **prosperity**. An **influx** of European **immigrants** brought foreign business and money into the country.

In 1929, the **Great Depression** caused economic collapse in countries all over the world, including Argentina. In 1930, a military government took control of the country.

Left:
Officials signed the papers that granted Argentina independence at the *cabildo* (cah-BEEL-doe), or town council, in Buenos Aires.

Left: Juan Perón's second wife, Evita Perón, worked to improve the lives of Argentines. She was dearly loved by the people. When she died in 1952, her coffin was carried through the streets, followed by the people in a **solemn** procession.

The Peróns

In 1946, Colonel Juan Perón became president. He was well liked by the working class. Perón **nationalized** industry and raised the minimum wage, but these changes caused **inflation** and other economic problems. After Perón left Argentina in 1955, many **ineffectual** leaders fought for power. In 1973, Perón returned and became president again. When he died in 1974, his third wife, Isabel, became president. Because she could not solve Argentina's economic problems, the military arrested her in 1976.

13

Military Rule and the 1980s

The military took over Argentina's government in 1976, and the "Dirty War" began. The Argentine military **abducted** and killed over ten thousand people for "anti-government activities."

Democracy was restored when Raúl Alfonsín was elected president in 1983. Carlos Saúl Menem was the next president. He solved many economic problems in Argentina. The current president is Fernando de la Rúa Bruno.

Above: The mothers of children who disappeared during the "Dirty War" demonstrate at the Plaza de Mayo every Thursday.

Justo José de Urquiza (1801–1870)

In 1853, Urquiza became president. Under his leadership, Argentina adopted a new constitution. Urquiza also opened the ports to world trade.

Juan Domingo Perón (1895–1974)

As Minister of Labor in the 1940s, Juan Perón reformed labor laws and gained the support of the working class. In 1946, he became president. In 1955, he fled to Spain to escape critics. He left Argentina with debts and high inflation. He was reelected president in 1973.

Juan Domingo Perón

María Estela (Isabel) Martínez de Perón (1931–)

Juan Perón's third wife, Isabel, became president when he died in 1974. She was the first woman president in the Americas.

María Estela (Isabel) Martínez de Perón

Government and the Economy

Argentina has twenty-three provinces and one **federal district** (Buenos Aires). The Argentine government is divided into three branches — executive, legislative, and judicial.

The president is the head of the executive branch and is elected to a four-year term. The legislative branch

Below: The Senate and the Chamber of Deputies are located in the Congress building.

16

is the National Congress, which is made up of the 72-member Senate and the 257-member Chamber of Deputies. The judicial branch operates the national and local court systems.

Above: Guards parade outside the Presidential Palace in Buenos Aires.

Elections

Voting is compulsory for people aged eighteen to seventy. Argentina has many political parties — some liberal and in favor of workers' rights, some conservative and in favor of the army.

Economy

Argentines have the highest incomes in Latin America. The standard of living in Argentina has greatly improved since the 1980s, when the economy suffered from high national debt and inflation.

Above: Pesticide is sprayed on crops to kill insects.

After President Menem's 1989 election, reforms brought some economic stability to Argentina. Now many goods are produced for export.

Agriculture is a major industry in Argentina, and 12 percent of the country's land is used to grow crops.

The fishing industry is also important to Argentina's economy. Over 700,000 tons of fish are caught each year. Ninety percent of the catch is exported, along with corn, wheat, and manufactured items, such as cars.

Above: Oil is one of Argentina's many natural resources.

Argentina has many natural resources. Gold, silver, and copper are mined in the Andes Mountains. Oil and natural gas are used locally and exported. Water power is gaining importance, so the government plans to build more **hydroelectric plants**.

People and Lifestyle

Argentina's population is about 36.7 million. The country is often called the "Nation of Immigrants" because about 4.5 million people in Argentina were born in another country.

About 85 percent of Argentines are of European descent. Before Spanish rule, many native Indians lived in Argentina, but most of them were killed by Spaniards. Today, **indigenous**

Below: A large part of the Argentine population has European roots.

people make up only 3 percent of the population. They live in Argentina's far northern and southern areas.

City and Country Lifestyles

Buenos Aires is home to over twelve million people. City dwellers are called *porteños* (por-TAY-nyos), meaning "people of the port." Porteños enjoy the excitement of city life, while, in the country, ranchers, farmers, and factory workers lead more down-to-earth lives.

Family

Families are close-knit in Argentina. About 69 percent of people between the ages of fourteen and twenty-nine live with their parents. Many young adults choose to live near their parents even after marriage.

The extended family also plays a major role. Grandparents, parents, and children often live under the same roof.

Below: Families spend quality time together at a park.

Families get together frequently with aunts, uncles, and cousins. The cousins often become close friends.

Above: Looks are very important to Argentine women. Recently, however, new roles have given women power that is not based on looks.

Argentine Women

Women in Argentina have struggled to improve their place in society. Evita Perón worked to increase the rights of women and, in 1947, helped women win the right to vote. In 1974, Isabel Perón became the first female president in the Americas. Today, women make up about 40 percent of the workforce.

Education

Argentina has one of the highest literacy rates in the world — 96 percent of the people can read. After seven years of required primary education, children can choose to go to a secondary school and then on to a university.

Over fifty universities can be found in Argentina. Twenty-four of them are funded by the government. The

Left: These girls have had a long day at their school in Argentina.

University of Buenos Aires is the largest university in Argentina. It is also one of the oldest.

Health and Social Security

The public health system in Argentina is very advanced. It is funded by both the government and private groups. Also, part of each worker's pay goes into a social security fund that provides full health care benefits.

Religion

Almost 90 percent of Argentines are registered as Catholics. For many years, only Catholics could be nominated as presidential candidates, but this law was dropped when the constitution was changed in 1994.

About 4 million Catholics make a **pilgrimage** to the city of Luján every year to pray to *La Virgen de Luján* (lah VEER-hen day loo-HAAN), the patron saint of Argentina.

Below: The tower of the church of San Francisco in Salta is believed to be the tallest in South America.

Judaism

Argentina has the largest Jewish community in Latin America. Jews make up about 2 percent of the population. Most of them live in Buenos Aires. In 1988, the Congress passed a law against **racism** and **anti-Semitism**, but Jewish people still face problems. In 1994, a bomb killed over one hundred people in a Jewish community center in Buenos Aires.

Above: These Catholics are making their way to a Sunday church service.

Language

The official language of Argentina is Spanish, but it is different from the dialects spoken in Spain. Argentine Spanish has its own sound.

Several other languages are spoken in Argentina. English is the country's second most popular language.

Below: A mime reads a newspaper.

Immigrants can also be heard speaking their native languages, such as French, German, and Italian. Another language called Lunfardo developed in the late 1800s among immigrants in Buenos Aires. Lunfardo is a mixture of Spanish and Italian, with some French, German, African, and Portuguese words.

Above: Jorge Luis Borges won worldwide acclaim with his books. He was nominated for the Nobel Prize for Literature several times.

Literature

Argentines love to read, and bookstores are found on every street corner. Famous Argentine authors include Adolfo Bioy Casares, Ernesto Sábato, and Victoria Ocampo, who greatly influenced Argentine literature.

Jorge Luis Borges was one of the most influential and famous writers in Argentina. Born in Buenos Aires in 1899, Borges wrote poetry, essays, and short stories. Another well-known Argentine writer was Manuel Puig. His book *Kiss of the Spider Woman* was made into a play and a movie.

Arts

During periods of political trouble in Argentina's history, the government banned several artists and their works. Today, Buenos Aires is the center of the arts in Argentina. Many museums in Buenos Aires feature Argentine art.

Silver Work

The name *Argentina* means "silver." Spanish explorers thought the land was

Below: A street performer "eats" fire to entertain and amaze the crowd.

rich in this mineral. In the 1700s, silversmiths came to Argentina from Europe and settled in Buenos Aires. Silver was often used to decorate Catholic churches, but most of this artwork was stolen in the wars that were fought during Spain's rule.

Today, beautiful silver work can be found throughout the country. The **gauchos** of the pampas use silver to make bridles and other useful items.

Painting

In the early years, wealthy immigrants from Europe bought paintings in Europe and sent them to Argentina. These Europeans also persuaded painters to come to Argentina and paint scenes of the new country. After a while, some Argentines became artists themselves.

Argentina's first national painter was Prilidiano Pueyrredón. He painted landscapes and portraits.

Left: A wall in the Cave of the Painted Hands in Santa Cruz province is covered with outlines of hand shapes. This painting is about two thousand years old.

Left: In the 1930s, Argentina's most famous **tango** singer, Carlos Gardel, starred in Hollywood movies. Gardel helped draw Hispanic audiences to the cinemas. His statue stands over his tomb, which attracts fans and tourists every year.

Cinema

The Argentine movie industry began at the end of World War I. In the second half of the 1900s, movies made in Argentina started gaining popularity.

Below: The tango is a famous dance from Argentina.

In 1976, Argentina came under military rule. Strict regulations were placed on movies, and the industry suffered. The situation improved when a democratic government took control in 1983. Some movies of the 1980s and 1990s were about the "Dirty War" and how it affected the Argentine people.

Leisure

Argentina's larger cities offer a wide range of leisure activities. Eating out, dancing, and attending cultural events are popular pastimes. Argentines also love watching and playing sports.

In Buenos Aires, people enjoy shopping on weekends. They also love to sit in *confiteriás* (con-fit-a-REE-as), or cafés, and watch the world go by.

Below: Argentines love to spend a leisurely afternoon sipping coffee at an outdoor café.

Left: During the summer months, Argentina's beaches are crowded with families out to enjoy the sun, sand, and sea.

Confiteriás are popular places for people to meet and relax. They read newspapers, play dominos or chess, or discuss politics and world events while sipping coffee or a cold drink.

During the summer, Argentines head for the beaches at resort towns, such as Mar del Plata and Pinamar. Besides water sports, these resort towns also offer horseback riding, golfing, tennis, gambling, and a vibrant nightlife.

Below: Hikers enjoy the outdoors on their way to Mount Fitzroy.

Sports

Argentina's variety of landscapes encourages many different sports. Snow sports are popular in Argentina, and people from all over the world travel to the Andes and attempt to climb Mount Aconcagua.

Above: Gabriela Sabatini rose to the top of the tennis world in the 1980s.

Tennis became popular in the 1970s and 1980s, when Guillermo Vilas and Gabriela Sabatini became star players. Other popular sports are auto racing, **polo**, and rugby, which is like football.

Fútbol

Soccer, or *fútbol* (FOOT-ball), has a huge following in Argentina. The Argentine national team won the World Cup Championship in 1978 and 1986.

The most famous Argentine soccer player is Diego Maradona, who was born in Buenos Aires. A goal he scored helped Argentina win the World Cup in 1986, and he was named Best Player for the entire tournament.

Above: Diego Maradona (*center*) is one of the best soccer players in the world. He was suspended in 1994 and returned to the game in 1996. He has since retired.

Opposite: Skiing is a popular sport in Argentina.

Festivals

The different regions in Argentina hold local festivals that attract people from all over the country.

Carnival

Carnival is a Catholic festival held just before the quiet time of Lent. Argentines, especially in the northern parts of the country, dress in elaborate costumes and parade noisily through the streets.

Wine Festival

Mendoza holds an annual week-long wine festival called *Vendimia* (ven-dee-MEE-a). Folk concerts and other events are held throughout the week, and thousands of visitors join in the festivities. During the festival, a bishop blesses the wine, a Wine Harvest Queen is crowned, and a large parade of musicians and floats fills the streets. The festivities end with a spectacular fireworks display.

Opposite: During Carnival, children dress up in bright, colorful costumes.

Below: During the Gaucho National Festival in San Antonio de Areco, dancers in traditional costumes perform folk dances.

Food

Argentina has only a few native dishes. Most of the country's cooking has come from the cultures of Europe. People in Argentina eat a lot of beef and love eating out in restaurants.

Argentines eat a light breakfast and have lunch after noon. Later in the afternoon, they have a light snack. Dinner is the biggest meal of the day. It is served late at night and sometimes lasts until midnight.

Below: Many Argentines enjoy a glass of wine with their meals.

Argentines eat beef every day. Argentina's cattle industry accounts for 5 percent of the country's exports.

A popular Argentine dish is *parrilla* (par-REE-zah), which is meat roasted over hot coals. Argentines also like meat grilled on a spit over hot coals. This method of cooking meat is called ***asado*** (ah-SAH-do).

41

BOLIVIA

PARAGUAY

Tropic of Capricorn

JUJUY

FORMOSA

SALTA

CHACO

Iguazú
Falls

Iguazú

TUCUMÁN

CATAMARCA

SANTIAGO
DEL
ESTERO

MISIONES

CORRIENTES

BRAZIL

LA RIOJA

SANTA FE

C
H
I
L
E

Paraná

Uruguay

SAN
JUAN

CÓRDOBA

ENTRE
RIOS

*Mount Aconcagua
(22,834 ft/6,960 m)*

SAN LUIS

URUGUAY

P
A
M
P
A
S

San Antonio
de Areco

■ BUENOS AIRES (FEDERAL DISTRICT)

MENDOZA

Luján

Rio de la Plata

**BUENOS
AIRES**

LA PAMPA

Pinamar

Mar del Plata

*ATLANTIC
OCEAN*

A
N
D
E
S

NEUQUÉN

RÍO NEGRO

Península Valdés

N

CHUBUT

P
A
T
A
G
O
N
I
A

SANTA
CRUZ

*Mount Fitzroy
(11,073 ft/3,375 m)*

ARGENTINA

TIERRA DEL FUEGO

Regional
Boundary

■ Capital

● City

River

Above: In 1936, the obelisk was built to commemorate the founding of Buenos Aires.

Andes B1–B4
Atlantic Ocean D3–D5

Bolivia B1
Brazil D1–D2
Buenos Aires
    (federal district) C2
Buenos Aires
    (province) C3

Catamarca B1
Chaco C1
Chile B1–B5
Chubut B4
Córdoba C2
Corrientes C2

Entre Ríos C2

Formosa C1

Gran Chaco C1

Iguazú Falls D1
Iguazú River D1

Jujuy B1

La Pampa B3–C3
La Rioja B2
Luján C2

Mar del Plata C3
Mendoza B2–B3
Mesopotamia
    C2–D1
Misiones D1
Mount Aconcagua
    B2
Mount Fitzroy B5

Neuquén B3

Pampas C2–C3
Paraguay C1

Paraná River C2
Patagonia B3–B5
Península Valdés C4
Pinamar C3

Río de la Plata C2
Río Negro B3

Salta B1–C1
San Antonio de
    Areco C2
San Juan B2

San Luis B2
Santa Cruz B4–B5
Santa Fe C2
Santiago del
    Estero C1

Tierra del Fuego
    B5–C5
Tucumán B1–C1

Uruguay D2
Uruguay River
    D1-D2

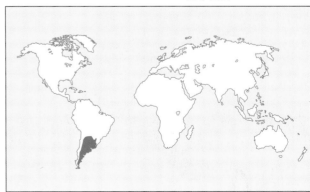

Quick Facts

Official Name   República Argentina, Argentine Republic

Capital   Buenos Aires

Official Language   Spanish

Population   36, 737, 664 (July 1999 estimate)

Land Area   1,073,518 square miles (2,780,412 sq km)

Provinces   Buenos Aires, Catamarca, Chaco, Chubut, Córdoba, Corrientes, Entre Ríos, Federal District, Formosa, Jujuy, La Pampa, La Rioja, Mendoza, Misiones, Neuquén, Río Negro, Salta, San Juan, San Luis, Santa Cruz, Santa Fe, Santiago del Estero, Tierra del Fuego, Tucumán

Highest Point   Mount Aconcagua (22,834 feet / 6,960 m)

Longest River   Paraná

Official Religion   Roman Catholicism

Important Festivals   Carnival, Easter, Festival de la Vendimia, the Gaucho Festival, Independence Day, May Revolution Day.

Currency   Peso (P $1.00 = U.S. $1 in 2000)

Opposite: Street artists are found all over Argentina.

Glossary

abducted: taken away illegally and in secret or by force; kidnapped.

anti-Semitism: prejudice against Jews.

asado (ah-SAH-do): a way of grilling meat on a spit, or stick, over hot coals. The gauchos made *asado* popular.

federal district: an area in which the national government of a country is located.

gauchos: Argentine cowboys who live on the pampas.

Great Depression: a period of world economic crisis that began with the U.S. stock market crash in 1929 and continued through most of the 1930s.

haven: a place of shelter and safety.

hydroelectric plants: power stations; places where electricity is produced using the power of moving water.

immigrants: people who move into a new country from another country.

indigenous: native to a country or geographic region; original.

ineffectual: incapable; failing to produce a satisfactory result.

inflation: an increase in the price of goods and services in a country.

influx: the arrival of people or things in large numbers; a flowing in.

nationalized: brought under the control of the nation or country.

Nobel laureates: people who received the Nobel Prize, a famous award for significant achievement in particular fields.

pampas: the grassy plains of central Argentina.

pilgrimage: a journey made to a sacred place as an act of religious devotion.

polo: a game between two teams of players on horseback who use long wooden sticks to hit a ball for a goal.

prosperity: success; wealth; a time of economic well-being.

quebracho (kay-BRA-cho): a tree with hard wood that grows in the Chaco region of Argentina.

racism: the belief that people of certain races are better or worse than others.

solemn: very serious.

tango: music and a dramatic ballroom dance that started in Argentina.

unique: one of a kind; unusual.

vibrant: lively; full of energy and color.

yerba mate (YAIR-ba MAH-tay): a type of energizing herbal tea.

More Books to Read

Argentina. Enchantment of the World second series. Martin Hintz (Children's Press)

Argentina. Globe-Trotters Club series. Suzanne Paul Dell'Oro (Carolrhoda Books)

Argentina. True Books series. Michael Burgan (Children's Press)

Argentina: A Wild West Heritage. Discovering Our Heritage series. Marge Peterson (Dillon Press)

Argentina, Chile, Paraguay, Uruguay. Country Fact Files series. Anna Selby (Raintree/Steck-Vaughn)

Argentina in Pictures. Visual Geography series. E. W. Egan (Lerner)

Buenos Aires. Cities of the World series. Deborah Kent (Children's Press)

The Magic Bean Tree: A Legend from Argentina. Nancy Van Laan (Houghton Mifflin Co.)

Maradona. Champion Sport Biographies series. Joseph Romain and Liam Goodall (Warwick)

The Tiniest Giants: Discovering Dinosaur Eggs. Lowell Dingus (Doubleday)

Videos

On Top of the World — Argentina. (Tapeworm)

Three Perfect Days: Buenos Aires. (Unapix)

Video Visits — Argentina, Land of Natural Wonder. (IVN Entertainment)

Web Sites

www.argentour.com/

www.buenosairestango.com

www.latinworld.com/sur/argentina/

www.pbs.org/edens/patagonia/

Due to the dynamic nature of the Internet, some web sites stay current longer than others. To find additional web sites, use a reliable search engine with one or more of the following keywords to help you locate information about Argentina. Keywords: *Argentina, Buenos Aires, gauchos, pampas, Patagonia, Evita Perón, tango.*

Index